I AM REA WORDS

by Jan Carr
cover illustration by Sandra Shap
illustrated by Theresa Fitzgerald

Scholastic Get Set Reading Skills Books are designed to help children understand that words are made up of sounds—and letters representing those sounds. Children are asked to add letters to make words they know, to read and write whole words, and to use words to complete sentences.

I Am Reading Words provides a comprehensive review of some of the first words children will recognize—words describing animals, clothing, and family members—as well as beginning sounds and rhymes. The lively stickers and varied activities reinforce these basic skills in a way that makes learning fun.

SCHOLASTIC INC.
New York Toronto London Auckland Sydney

TO THE PARENT:

- Set aside a special time and place to work with your child. Your interest communicates that reading is both valuable and enjoyable.
- Help your child read the word lists at the beginning of each activity. You may want to read each word out loud yourself and have your child read it after you.
- Make sure the directions on each page are clear to your child.
- Be sensitive to the pace at which your child works and learns. Remember that some pages may be a lot of work and can be completed at another time. The activities should be fun. If at any point they start to become frustrating, for your child *or* for you, put them aside until another time.
- Encourage your child's verbal participation as much as possible. Use the pages as jumping-off points for conversation and related discussion.
- Reward good work with praise and liberal use of reward stickers. Your involvement in the learning process will help your child GET SET to read!

STICKER INSTRUCTIONS
Carefully punch out stickers.
Moisten them and put on pages where they belong.

Rewards!
Use these stickers on any page.

ISBN 0-590-42734-2

Copyright © 1989 by Scholastic Inc. All rights reserved. Published by Scholastic Inc.

12 11 10 9 8 7 6 5 4 3 2 1   8 9/8 0 1 2 3/9

Printed in the U.S.A.   11

First Scholastic printing, November 1989

Animals at the Zoo

Read the words in the word list.
Draw a line from each word to the correct animal.

monkey

kangaroo

bear

lion

seal

giraffe

elephant

Give the monkey a banana sticker.

Colorful Words

Read the words in the word list.

red   blue   green   yellow   purple
black   white   brown   orange

Color the apple red.

Color the witch's hat black.

Color the sun yellow.

Color the plum purple.

Color the blue jay blue.

Color the cow brown.

Color the lettuce green.

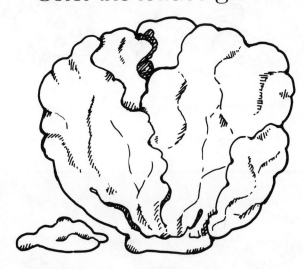

Color the orange orange.

Color the snowflake white.

What color are the stickers?
Find the sticker with the right
word and put it here.

Numbers I Can Count

Read the words in the word list.

one   two   three   four   five

Look at the pictures below.
Count the objects.
Write the word for each number.
Some of the words are started for you.

1
house

_____

on - - - - - - - - - - - - - - - - - -

2
fish

_____

- -

3
cats

_____

- - - - - - - - - - - - - - - - - - - -

_____

4
hats

_____

f o - - - - - - - - - - - - - - - -

_____

Find a sticker that has
five things on it.
Paste it next to the number five.

5
stars

_____

- - - - - - - - - - - - - - - - - - - -

_____

6

Family Words

Read the words in the word list.

**mother   father   sister   brother
grandmother   grandfather**

Everyone's family is different.
Draw a picture of your family below.
Write each person's name underneath his or her picture.

Find the sticker with the family of kittens.
Paste it here.

Words Around the House

Read the words in the word list.

cat   flowers   sun   bowl   rug   lamp

Look at the picture.
Use the word list to fill in the missing words in the sentences below.

The _____ is on the chair.

The _____ are in the vase.

The spoon is next to the _____ .

The table is on the _____ .

The _____ is on the table.

Find the sun sticker.
Put it in the window.
Finish the sentence below.

The _____ is in the window.

Beginning Letters

Read the words in the word list.

cow book frog house kite
monkey tree five nest

Draw a line from each picture
to the letter that starts the word.

c p s b l f h m j k m y n t f o r n

Find the sticker that says K.
Paste it on the kite.

9

C is for Circus!

Read the words in the word list.

clown   car   club   can   camel

All the words begin with C.
Find all the C words in the picture below.
Color them in.

Find the cat sticker.
Paste it on top of the camel.

Dot-to-Dot Ds

Read the words in the word list.

dog   dress   desk   dots

Look at the picture.
Find the words that begin with D.
Someone has snuck into class.
Connect the dots to find out who it is.

dress

dog

dots

desk

Find the sticker with the dog dish.
Paste it near the dog.

Beginning Sounds

Say the sound sh-.
Read the words in the word list.

**sheep   shoes   shirt   ship   shadow
shell   sheriff   shorts**

All the words begin with the blend sh-.
Look at the picture.
Circle each thing in the picture that
begins with sh-.

Paste the shark sticker by the ship.
Paste the shield sticker on the sheriff.

Blending In

Read the words in the word list.

stop star brush broom fly train
tree truck chair chicken three thumb

Each word begins with a blend.
Say the sounds of each blend below.
In each row, circle the pictures
whose names begin with the right blend.

st

br

fl

tr

ch

th

Find a sticker that starts with the sound fl-.
Paste it in the empty space.

Words for Clothes

Read the words in the word list.

hat   shirt   pants   socks   shoes

Find the words in the puzzle below.
Look across and down.
Circle the words.

```
Q  S  J  N  V  P
S  H  I  R  T  A
Z  O  B  F  G  N
U  E  L  H  A  T
K  S  O  C  K  S
```

Find the hat sticker.
Put it on the boy.

Winter Clothes

Read the words in the word list.

cap   mittens   coat   boots

What is missing?
Write the word.

A _____ .
Draw it into the picture.

Find the snowman sticker.
Paste it next to the girl.

Words for Fruits

Read the words in the word list.
Then fill in the puzzle below.

grapes   apple   pear   peach

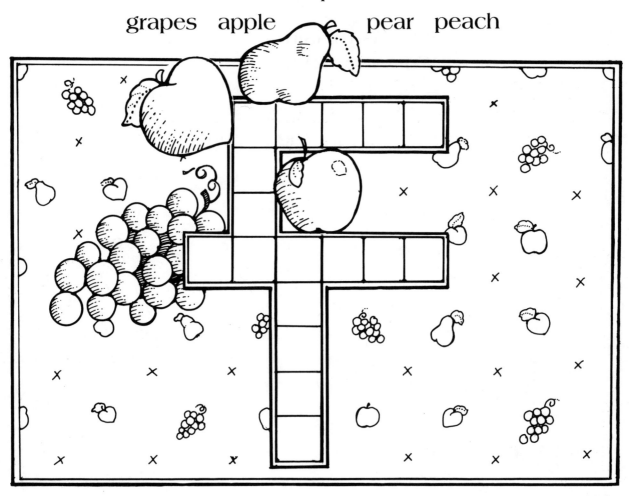

Find four fruit stickers.
Put them in the basket.

Words for Vegetables

Read the words in the word list.

peas   lettuce   beans   carrot

Find these words in the picture.
Color them in.

VEGETABLE · STAND

Find two vegetable stickers.
Add them to the stand.

Scrambled Eggs

Read the words in the word list.

egg   chicken   barn   nest

The words in the picture are scrambled.
Write the real words in the spaces below.
Draw a line from each word
to the right part of the picture.

tnse

——— ——— ———

rbna

——— ——— ———

geg

——— ——— ———

ckihenc

——— ——— ——— ———

Who hatches out of the egg?
Find the right sticker.
Paste it over the egg.

Some Words Are Opposites

Read the words in the word list.

short tall black white
slow fast young old

Finish each sentence by writing the correct word in the empty space.

The tree is _____.   short

The flower is _____.   tall

The dog is _____.   black

The cat is _____.   white

The horse is _____.   slow

The turtle is _____.   fast

The baby is _____.   young

The grandfather is _____.   old

Find a sticker with opposites on it.
Put the sticker here.

Where Is It?

Read the words in the word list.

in under over around

Look at the pictures.
Draw a circle around the right word.

The girl put the boat   in   the tub.
                        under

The boy walks   over   the house.
                around

The horse jumps   over   the fence.
                  under

The girl hid the box   around   her bed.
                       under

Who is in the box?
Paste the sticker here.

Some Words Have the Same Ending

Say the sound -ug.
Read the words in the word list.

bug hug jug rug

These words all have the same ending.
Fill in the missing letters.

_____ug

_____ug

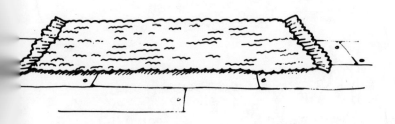

_____ug

_____ug

Give the bug a mug sticker.

Words That End in -oon.

Say the sound -oon.
Read the words in the word list.

moon   spoon   balloon   raccoon

These words all have the same ending.
Help the raccoon find the balloon.

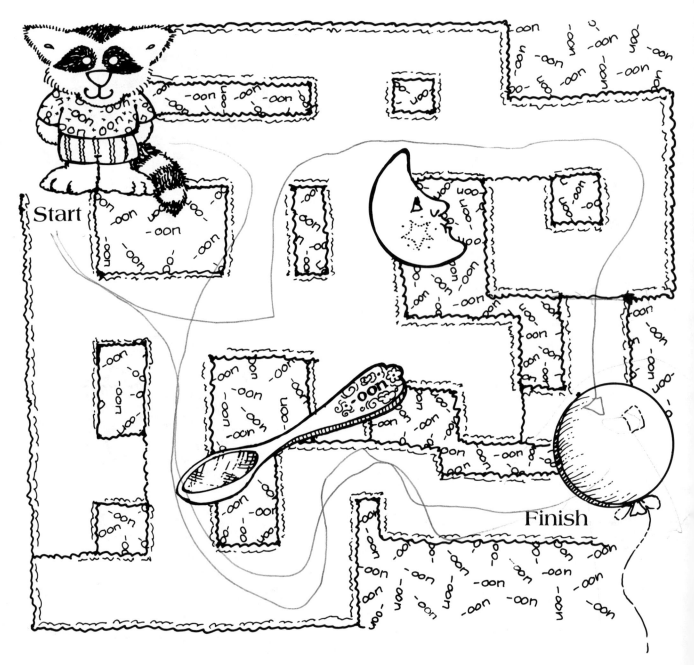

Start

Finish

Paste a balloon sticker over the balloon.

-ar Words

Say the sound -ar.
Read the words in the word list.

car   star   jar   guitar

These words all have the same ending.
Fill in the missing letters.

___ar

___ ___ar

___ar

___ ___ ___ ___ar

Put the star sticker over the star.

Words That End in -ook.

Say the sound -ook.
Read the words in the word list.

book   hook   cook   crook

These words have the same ending.
Circle all the -ook words below.

dragon   rocket   hook   bus

crook   door   rabbit   trumpet

umbrella   drum   whale   book

skates   cook   bird   lamp

Find a sticker that matches one of the -ook words.
Paste it on top of the word.

Rhyming Pairs

Read the words in the word list.

can fan hen ten map cap
king ring bee tree

In each group below, two of the words rhyme.
Draw a line between the rhyming words.

Give the hen a pen sticker.

Rhyming Sentences

Read the words in the word list.

pan   bell   snake   sad   jail

Read the sentences below.
Fill in the missing words.

The man picked up the _____ .

The _____ fell in the well.

The _____ is eating the cake.

The dad is feeling _____ .

The snail is in the _____ .

Give the snail a pail sticker.

More Rhymes

Read the words in the word list.

moo   boo   canoe   you

These words rhyme.
Use the word list to finish the sentences below.

The cow says _____.

The ghost says _____.

They paddle a _____.

How about _____?

More than two
can steer this canoe.
Add a kangaroo
and a cockatoo.
When you find the right stickers,
let them ride, too.

Some Words Are Compound Words

Some words are made up of two words.
They are called compound words.
Read the words in the word list.

sunglasses   rainbow   doghouse   ladybug   earring

Draw a line from each pair of pictures
to the picture of the word they make.

Find two stickers to put together
to make a compound word.
Paste them here.

More Compound Words

Read the words in the word list.

**football   swordfish   fingernail
sunflower   cupcake   rattlesnake**

In each group, two words can make a compound word.
Draw a circle around the two words
that can go together.

Paste a sunshine sticker on the sun.

Words I Can Read

apple
around

balloon
barn
beans
bear
bee
bell
black
blue
boo
book
boots
bowl
broom
brother
brown
brush
bug

camel
can
canoe
cap
car

carrot
cat
chair
chicken
clown
club
coat
cook
cow
crook
cupcake

desk
dog
doghouse
dots
dress

earring
egg
elephant

fan
fast
father

fingernail
five
flowers
fly
football
four
frog

giraffe
grandfather
grandmother
grapes
green
guitar

hat
hen
hook
house
hug

in

jail
jar
jug

kangaroo
king
kite

ladybug
lamp
lettuce
lion

map
mittens
monkey
moo
moon
mother

nest

old
one
orange
over

pan
pants

peach
pear
peas
purple

raccoon
rainbow
rattlesnake
red
ring
rug

sad
seal
shadow

sheep
shell
sheriff
ship
shirt
shoes
short
shorts
sister
slow
snake
socks
spoon
star
stop

sun
sunflower
sunglasses
swordfish

tall
ten
three
thumb
train
tree
truck
two

under

white

yellow
you
young

Congratulations!

You know lots of new words.
Draw a picture of yourself.

Find the prize ribbon sticker.
Give yourself first prize.